Graphic design and illustrations: Zapp

Story adaptation: Jane Brierley

© 1996 Tormont Publications Inc.
   338 Saint Antoine St. East
   Montreal, Canada H2Y 1A3
   Tel. (514) 954-1441
   Fax (514) 954-5086

Printed in China

THE WILD SWANS

TORMONT

$\mathcal{O}$nce upon a time, there lived a king who had eleven sons and one daughter named Elise. The children loved each other very much and were very close. They lived in a beautiful castle, but they played and studied just like children from any large, happy family. Sadly, their mother had died shortly after the last little prince was born.

$\mathcal{A}$s time went on, the king got over the sadness of his wife's death. He met a beautiful woman and fell in love. He asked her to become his queen, not knowing that she was really a witch.

"I will have a loving companion, and my children will have a mother once again," he thought to himself. But as soon as she set foot in the castle, the new queen hated the children and resolved to get rid of them.

The queen began telling lies to turn the king against his children. Then, early one morning, she gathered the princes along the castle wall.

"Go!" she ordered. "You shall wander the world with nothing but your wings to help you."

And with a wave of her cloak, she turned them into wild swans – but because they were princes, each had a gold crown on his head.

The wicked queen told the king that she had seen the princes running away from the castle. "Let the ungrateful wretches go," she said. Then she sent Elise to live with a peasant family, telling the king that his daughter needed to be with other children.

When Elise turned fifteen, the king decided to send for her. The queen pretended to welcome her kindly. "Come my dear," she said. "You must get ready to meet your father."

$\mathscr{W}$hile Elise undressed for her bath, the queen used her magic to summon three huge toads. She picked them up, one by one, and gave each a kiss and a command. "I want you to sit on Elise's head and make her stupid. You shall lie near her heart and harden it, and you shall hop onto her forehead and make her ugly." Then she threw the toads into the bath, and soon the water turned a sickly green.

But Elise's innocence and sweetness broke the witch's spell. The toads turned into scarlet poppies, and the water became as clear as crystal.

The queen flew into a rage. She grabbed the girl, rubbed walnut juice on her face, and tied knots in her hair.

When Elise appeared before the king, he was shocked and angry. "This child is not my daughter!" he exclaimed.

"Father! It's me, Elise!" cried the poor girl.

"Ha! A dirty wretch who's after your gold!" snorted the queen.

"Take her away!" the king ordered.

$\mathcal{P}$oor Elise crept away into the forest, brokenhearted. She missed her brothers more than ever and longed to hear of them. As she sat by a stream, washing her face and untangling her hair, an old woman appeared behind her.

"Have you ever seen eleven princes wandering about?" asked Elise hopefully.

"No, my dear child, but I have seen eleven swans with little gold crowns on their heads," the old woman replied. "They often come to the water's edge at dusk." She pointed through the woods to a large lake.

$\mathcal{E}$lise ran to the shore and waited. At sunset, she heard the beating of wings, and, sure enough, down from the sky came eleven wild swans wearing crowns. At first, Elise was frightened and hid behind a rock.

One by one, the swans swooped down to the shore. As they landed, they shook off their feathers. Watching from her hiding place, Elise was amazed to discover that they were her brothers!

"Anton, Sebastian, it's me, Elise!" she cried, calling out their names as she ran into their arms. The brothers could hardly believe their eyes and ears as they gathered around their long lost sister.

What a happy reunion it was! The brothers told Elise how the wicked witch had cast a spell on them, and she explained how she had been banished from the castle.

"We are swans by day, and become human at sunset," explained Anton, the oldest brother.

"I will find a way to save you," Elise assured them. "But in the meantime, please don't leave me."

$\mathscr{T}$he brothers found a large piece of cloth
for Elise to lie on. Then, as the sun rose and
the princes turned back into swans, they gently
lifted her up and flew away. Sebastian, the
youngest, dropped berries into her lap for food.
By sunset, they had reached a secret cave in a
far-off forest.

That night, Elise dreamed of a fairy flying above her on a leaf.

"You can break the spell if you are prepared to suffer," whispered the fairy. "You must collect stinging nettles from a graveyard and knit eleven shirts from their soft flax. When you have finished them all, throw them over your brothers and the spell will be broken. But beware — until you are finished you must not speak or laugh."

"I don't care!" cried Elise in her dream. "I'll do anything to save my brothers!"

$\mathcal{W}$hen Elise awoke, it was morning and her brothers had gone. On the floor beside her lay a huge pile of sharp nettles. She set to work at once. By the time the princes returned to the cave, they found Elise knitting a curious garment. Her hands were scratched and her fingers were blistered from making the flax.

"What are you doing?" asked Sebastian. But Elise could say nothing.

$\mathcal{T}$ears rose in Sebastian's eyes as he bent over his sister to watch her work. The tears spilled onto her fingers, and at once the blisters disappeared. She smiled at him gratefully, but dared not speak or laugh.

The brothers watched for a while. The whole thing was so mysterious that they began to understand that some kind of magic was at work. Perhaps Elise was trying to save them.

$\mathcal{E}$arly the next morning, after the brothers had flown away, Elise stepped outside the cave. "I'll take my work and sit in that leafy oak," she thought. "No one will see me there."

Before long, however, a group of hunters spotted her. "Who are you, girl?" they shouted roughly. When she didn't respond, they dragged her down from the tree.

"Stop!" cried a voice, and a young king came riding up.

"What is your name?" asked the young king, kindly. Elise just shook her head and smiled. "She shall come with me," said the king, dismissing the hunters.

They returned to his castle. The king tried speaking to Elise in several languages, all the while watching her knit. Although she said nothing, her gentle glance and lovely face captured the king's heart.

$\mathcal{E}$lise now lived in luxury, but still she spent most of her time knitting quietly. The king often sat with her, and found happiness in her company. At last he spoke to the archbishop. "I love this sweet maiden and I mean to marry her," he announced.

The archbishop was horrified. "You know nothing about the girl! She could be a witch, for all we know. What about her strange knitting?"

But the king was determined. He spoke to Elise, who clasped his hand lovingly, but still kept silent. They were married soon after.

$\mathcal{E}$lise continued knitting until she had no more nettles left. That night, she went to pick nettles from a graveyard. A group of witches had gathered there, but Elise cared only about her brothers' shirts.

Meanwhile, the archbishop ran to get the king. "Your wife is up to no good!" he warned.

The king followed him, and to his horror found Elise crouching on the ground, while three hideous witches cackled over a nearby grave.

"I can't believe it!" cried the brokenhearted king. "Do what you must."

$\mathcal{E}$lise was accused of witchcraft.

"Wife, say you are innocent, I beg you,"

pleaded the king. But Elise could only gaze at him sadly.

The next morning, she was taken to the market square to be burnt at the stake. She was still knitting, and beside her lay a pile of ten shirts. As the cart passed through the crowd, the angry mob shouted "Burn the Witch!"

Suddenly, the sky grew dark as eleven wild swans swooped down beside her. Quickly, she threw the shirts over them. The crowd gasped as the great swans turned into princes.

Sebastian, who got the eleventh shirt with only one sleeve, still had one wing.

"Save me!" Elise cried out at last. "I'm innocent!"

$\mathscr{E}$lise, surrounded by her brothers, went up to the king. Tears of joy fell from her eyes as she told the story of the spell cast by her wicked stepmother, how she had found her brothers once more, and why she had kept silent while knitting the nettle shirts.

The king also wept for joy and clasped his wife tenderly. "My darling, only someone with your goodness of heart would make such a sacrifice."

$\mathcal{T}$he crowd cheered "God bless the queen!"
Then Elise noticed Sebastian's wing. "Oh, your
poor arm!" she cried in distress.

"Don't be sad" he said, hugging her. "I will
carry my swan's wing proudly, as the symbol of
a sister's unselfish love."